For God so loved the world,
that He gave His only Son,
that whoever believes in Him
should not perish
but have eternal life.

✳ ✳ ✳ ✳ ✳

John 3:16

Copyright © 2008 by Concordia Publishing House
3558 S. Jefferson Avenue, St. Louis, MO 63118-3968
1-800-325-3040 • www.cph.org

Manufactured in China.

1 2 3 4 5 6 7 8 9 10   17 16 15 14 13 12 11 10 09 08

The Christmas List

By Susan K. Leigh

✳ ✳ ✳ ✳ ✳

Illustrated by Alan Flinn

CONCORDIA PUBLISHING HOUSE • SAINT LOUIS

$Jacob$ stood near the window, waiting. As soon as the car pulled in the driveway, he shouted, "She's here!"

Grandma was visiting that evening. That meant Jacob and Emily could stay up later than usual. Grandma always brought special treats, like Emily's favorite cut out cookies or Jacob's favorite homemade caramel popcorn. And she always told funny stories about their dad when he was a little boy.

At dinner, Jacob told Grandma about scouts and basketball. Emily told her about piano lessons and the school field trip to the science museum.

Then Grandma asked what was on their Christmas lists.

Jacob had his list in his pocket. "I want a new computer game and a baseball glove and a microscope and walkie talkies and a model airplane and a skateboard and ..." He had a long list.

"What about you, Emily?"

Emily was quiet for a long moment. Then she said, "I don't have a list yet."

"You have to hurry," Jacob told her. "Christmas is almost here."

His words bothered Emily. She looked down at her plate, not certain what to say.

Jacob tried to be helpful. "What about a new bicycle? Your old bike is almost too small."

"Maybe," Emily said. "But my old bike is purple, and purple is my favorite color."

"Or a new doll," Jacob said. "You like the one in the catalog that came yesterday."

Yes, Emily very much liked the doll in the catalog. "But I like the one I got for my birthday more. She's my favorite," she said.

Grandma suggested board games or books or a sleeping bag.

Those were all good ideas and Emily agreed that they would be very nice presents. But she wasn't sure she wanted any of them enough to put them on her Christmas list.

Grandma squeezed her hand. "That's okay, Em. You don't have to decide now."

After dinner, they watched the movie Grandma had brought. Jacob enjoyed it a lot and laughed at all the funny parts. But Emily couldn't pay much attention to it. She was thinking.

What if she couldn't decide what she wanted for Christmas? What if she didn't make a list? What would happen if she made a list but put things on it that she wasn't sure she liked? If she made a mistake, would she get something she didn't want?

These were troubling questions.

At bedtime, Grandma made sure they brushed their teeth and listened as they said their prayers. Then she tucked them in and kissed each of them on the forehead. "Good night, Jacob. Good night, Emily. God bless you and keep you," she said.

Emily didn't go right to sleep though. She lay awake, still thinking about her Christmas list.

But the next morning, Emily was in a happy mood. On Sundays, Dad made pancakes, and Emily loved pancakes!

"Did you have fun last night?" Mom asked.

Jacob nodded and answered, "Yes! We watched a funny movie and I had caramel popcorn."

Emily nodded too. "Grandma listened to our prayers and tucked us in."

Then Jacob said, "I gave Grandma my Christmas list, but Emily doesn't have one."

"What's this?" Dad asked. "No Christmas list?"

Emily slowly shook her head. "I haven't made my list yet."

"You have to hurry," Jacob told her. "Christmas is almost here."

Mom told Jacob to finish his breakfast, then she kissed the top of Emily's head. "There's plenty of time to make your list, Em."

"But there isn't plenty of time this morning," Dad said. "We need to get ready for church and Sunday School."

In Sunday School, Mrs. Miller, her teacher, told the class about the Christmas story.

"The governor had a list of all the people he ruled. This list was called a 'census.' Joseph and Mary went to Bethlehem to be registered for the census by adding their name to the governor's list.

"Our church has another kind of list," Mrs. Miller said. "This is a list of families in our town who are needy. Our class is collecting Christmas gifts for the children in one of these families."

Emily already knew the Christmas story and she already knew about the toy drive. But Mrs. Miller's words caused her to wonder about something.

She raised her hand. "Teacher, does God have a list too?"

Mrs. Miller thought for a moment,
then replied, "Yes, God has a list. He created us,
so He knows everything about us, what we say and do,
what we think and how we feel, even how many hairs
we have on our heads. We are His children.

"But sometimes we don't behave like His children.
We sin. That's why God sent His Son, Jesus. Jesus was
born at Christmas to bring us forgiveness for our sins.
He did that when He died on the cross.

"Now, everyone who believes Jesus
is our Savior is on God's list. This is
called His 'Book of Life,' and it has
the names of all the people who will
be with Him in heaven one day."

Emily thought about God's list all the way home and during lunch. She imagined what it might look like and how long it might be.

That afternoon, they went to the store to get gifts for the church toy drive. Emily and Jacob looked at every toy in every aisle. Jacob picked out a car to give, but Emily couldn't make up her mind. She remembered the things she had at home and the things on Jacob's Christmas list. And she remembered what her teacher had said in Sunday School.

Then Emily knew what she wanted to give for the toy drive. And she knew what to put on her Christmas list.

When they got home, Emily went to her room. She worked on her Christmas list until Mom called her for supper.

It was Jacob's turn to say grace: "Now we bow our heads to pray; thank You for this food today. Now we fold our hands and say, 'Thank You, Lord, in every way.' Amen."

"What were you doing all afternoon?" Mom asked Emily.

"I was making my Christmas list," she answered.

"Finally!" Jacob said. "What's on it?"

Emily pulled a piece of paper from her pocket and unfolded it once, twice, three times. Then she turned the paper around so everyone else could see.

There were no words written on it. There was just a big red heart in the center of the page. And in the center of the heart was a cross.

"You want a heart for Christmas?" Jacob asked. "What kind of present is that?"

"It stands for love," Emily explained. "In Sunday School, we learned that Joseph and Mary put their names on the governor's list. And we learned that God has a list called the 'Book of Life.' My teacher says this is a list of people who will be with Jesus in heaven.

Emily continued, "What I want for Christmas is for all children everywhere to know about Jesus. So I'm going to start telling them by giving my favorite Bible story book for the toy drive."

Mom smiled, and Dad nodded his head.

"Because," Emily said, "God's list is the best kind of Christmas list ever."

For God so loved the world,
that He gave His only Son,
that whoever believes in Him
should not perish
but have eternal life.

✳ ✳ ✳ ✳ ✳

John 3:16